Praise for *Medea*

"Robertson is master of the dark and wounded, the torn complexities of human relations, and *Medea* offers a perfect match for his sensibilities. This is an urgent, contemporary, and eloquent translation."

—A.L. Kennedy, winner of the 2007 Costa Book of the Year

"The greatest works demand constant re-translation to meet the changing culture of the age, and Robin Robertson has given us a *Medea* fit for our times; his elegant and lucid free translation of Euripides' masterpiece manages the trick of sounding wholly contemporary but never merely 'modern'—and will be an especially lucky discovery for those encountering the play for the first time."

—Don Paterson, winner of the T. S. Eliot Prize and the Whitbread Poetry Award

"Robin Robertson is a fine poet and one well-matched to the task of making an English version of Euripides' great play. The tough but musical vernacular line he has found brings home the brutality and ineffable sadness of *Medea* in a way that seems perfectly pitched for a modern audience."

—David Harsent, winner of the Forward Poetry Prize, Fellow of the British Royal Society of Literature

*f*P

Also by Robin Robertson

EURIPIDES

MEDEA

A NEW TRANSLATION BY
Robin Robertson

FREE PRESS

New York London Toronto Sydney

FREE PRESS

A Division of Simon & Schuster, Inc.

1230 Avenue of the Americas

New York, NY 10020

First Free Press trade paperback edition October 2009

FREE PRESS and colophon are trademarks of Simon & Schuster, Inc.

For information about special discounts for bulk purchases,
please contact Simon & Schuster Special Sales at 1-866-506-1949
or business@simonandschuster.com

The Simon & Schuster Speakers Bureau can bring authors
to your live event. For more information or to book an event
contact the Simon & Schuster Speakers Bureau at
1-866-248-3049 or visit our website at www.simonspeakers.com

Manufactured in the United States of America

3   5   7   9   10   8   6   4

Library of Congress Cataloging-in-Publication Data

Euripides. Medea / Euripides; translated by Robin Robertson.
p. cm.
1. Medea (Greek mythology)--Drama. I. Robertson, Robin,
II. Title: Medea. English. III. Title.
PA3975.M4R63 2008
882'.01--dc22   2008006655

ISBN 978-1-4165-9223-5
ISBN 978-1-4165-9225-9 (pbk)

to Clare

"Your name means 'healer,'" she said. "Well, heal this,"
drawing back the red sheet and showing me
our two dead sons, full of wounds.

CONTENTS

INTRODUCTION

EURIPIDES

We know next to nothing about Euripides: an approximate date of birth—485–480 BC—and a probable date of death—407 or 406 BC. It is thought he was born on the island of Salamis, west of Athens, and that he spent most of his life in the township of Phyla, north of Mount Hymettus, near the capital, and that he died in Macedonia.

The one accurate ancient source we have is the *Didaskalia*: a compilation of Aristotle's lists of the plays produced at the Dionysian festival in Athens. This provides the names of the dramatists, the plays, the principal actors and the prizes awarded. Euripides is recorded as the author of ninety-two plays (of which only nineteen survive) but he won the first prize only four times, and once posthumously. Whether this was due to the high quality of the contemporary competition or Athenian hostility to his work is hard to say.

The life of Euripides coincided with the great period of Athenian culture, when the empire was consolidated and the city was established as the cultural hub of the Greek-speaking world. Beginning with the Greek defeat of the invading Persians at Marathon (490 BC) and Salamis (480 BC), this fertile half-century ended with the outbreak of the Peloponnesian War in 431 BC, the year *Medea* was first performed. This war between Athens and

Sparta lasted twenty-seven years and ended in Athenian defeat in 404 BC. At some time between the catastrophic naval campaign in Sicily (415–413 BC) and the end of the war, Euripides left Athens for voluntary exile in Macedonia. Tradition has it that he met a grotesquely violent end: torn apart either by dogs (like Actaeon) or women—like Pentheus in his last extant play, the *Bacchae*.

GREEK TRAGEDY

In the fifth century BC, epic poetry was the conventional art form and tragedy was a relatively recent Athenian invention, originating—according to Aristotle—in the dithyrambs (choral songs in honor of Dionysus). The three great exponents of the new form were Aeschylus, Sophocles and Euripides, and they quickly established the ground rules: a mythological subject matter that used the tight focus of the family (and its associated duties and transgressions, loves and loathings) to open out wider civic implications in the state—while still allowing the drama to fall, in the end, under the inevitable sway of the gods.

STAGING

Medea was first performed in the huge open-air theater of Dionysus on the south slope of the Athenian acropolis, as part of a competitive drama festival held every spring, in honor of the god, before an audience of between 15,000 and 20,000 people, predominantly male, sitting in the semicircular rows of stepped seats in the *theatron*. There was a raised wooden stage, at the back of which was a single-story stage building, a *skênê*, representing a house, temple or palace, with a large circular area below, known as the *orchêstra*, where the Chorus sang and danced. There were three points of entry to the acting area: from the *skênê*, and from two entrances—or *eisodoi*—to the right and left of the stage. The dramatists also had two mechanical features at their disposal: the *ekkyklêma*, a wheeled platform on which a tableau of actors could be grouped, and the *mêchanê*, a crane on which a god could arrive or depart. This latter *deus ex machina* provides the dramatic finale to *Medea*.

There were usually three speaking actors, who were all male, and masked; the masks allowing them to assume different characters. The Chorus, made up of twelve to fifteen performers (again, all male), had an importance in Greek tragedy that is now largely lost to us. The Chorus had a central role: their dancing and their sung choral odes provided not just a counterpoint to the drama, but some of the finest lyric poetry. They represented the decent objective view: fellow citizens and interested spectators, offering an ethical and religious commentary on the action of the play. We find their relatives in Shakespeare, in moral touchstones such as Enobarbus in *Antony and Cleopatra* or Kent in *King Lear*. Almost all the action took place offstage and was reported by an eyewitness or messenger, then reflected on by the Chorus.

JASON AND MEDEA

Athenian audiences were extremely sophisticated and would have been familiar with the full arc of the myth of Jason and Medea. The hero's voyage in search of the Golden Fleece is familiar, but it is worth rehearsing the full narrative—and the lesser-known conclusions to the legends.

Jason's father, Aeson, had his rightful place on the throne of Iolcos usurped by his half-brother, Pelias. At Jason's birth his parents, fearing for his life, told Pelias that their child was stillborn, while sending him into the care of Chiron the centaur on Mount Pelion. When he came of age, Jason set off on his journey home to Iolcos. On the way, he helped an old woman across a river, losing one of his sandals in the process. The woman was the goddess Hera in disguise, and by his help he won her protection. Meanwhile, Pelias had been told by an oracle that he would be killed by a man wearing a single sandal.

When the young man arrived at Iolcos to claim his birthright he was recognized as such by Pelias, who asked Jason what he would do if an oracle told him that a particular man would kill him. Jason replied that he would send such a man in search of the legendary Golden Fleece of Colchis: an impossible, lethal undertaking. Pelias duly made this a condition.

Jason, the impetuous youth eager for glory, assembled a crew of heroes for the *Argo*. After many adventures they arrived in Colchis. The king, Aeëtes, told Jason that he would only give him the fleece if he fulfilled certain tasks: yoking the fire-breathing bulls to plough a field, sowing the dragon's teeth and dealing with the warriors that would spring from that seed. Hera made Medea, the sorceress daughter of Aeëtes, fall in love with Jason and assist him; Medea did so, using her magic to bewitch the serpent guarding the Golden Fleece. Having taken the prize, the Argonauts and Medea then fled Colchis, with the furious Aeëtes in pursuit. To slow the pursuers, Medea murdered her brother, Apsyrtus, dismembered the corpse, then fed it piecemeal into the wake of the *Argo*. Aeëtes had to stop and retrieve his son's remains, allowing Jason and his crew to escape.

Returning at last to Iolcos, and now married to Medea, Jason discovered that his father had been killed by Pelias and that the city stood heavily defended against attack. Medea told the ship's company that she would take revenge—and the city—single-handedly. Disguising herself as the goddess Artemis, she persuaded Pelias that she had rejuvenating powers. She cut up an old ram and boiled the pieces in a cauldron with magic herbs, then released a frisky lamb she had hidden in her costume. Pelias was convinced, and Medea charmed him to sleep. She then told his three daughters that, in order to make their father young again, they must cut him up, just as they had seen her do with the ram, and boil the pieces in the same cauldron. They followed her instructions, only to discover that Medea had tricked them into murdering their father.

The brutality of this act caused public outrage, and Jason and Medea were forced to flee Iolcos, settling in Corinth and starting a family. It is at this point that the action of *Medea* begins.

As suggested in the final scene of the play, Medea escaped from Corinth and found sanctuary with King Aegeus in Athens and gave him the son, Medus, he had craved. However, many years earlier, Aegeus had slept with Aethra, daughter of Bellerophon. He told her that if she gave birth to a son he should be raised secretly in Troezen. If the boy grew strong enough to move the rock under which Aegeus had hidden his sword and sandals then he was to be sent with them to Athens. The boy, whose name was Theseus, was indeed strong enough and, after his many labors on the coast road from Troezen to Athens, he arrived in the city of his father. Aegeus did not recognize him, of course, but Medea did—and knew him as a threat to her son Medus and his succession to the throne. She offered Theseus a cup of poisoned wine but, just as he was about to drink it, the king recognized the elaborate carving on the hilt of Theseus' sword and dashed the cup from his lips.

After being banished from Athens, Medea traveled widely—teaching snake-charming, it is said, in Italy, entering beauty contests in Thessaly—before marrying an Asian king. She later re-established herself in Colchis, killing her uncle Perses and restoring her father Aeëtes to the throne. Nothing is known of her death. Some say that she, rather than Helen, married Achilles; others claim that she never died, but became an immortal and ruled the Elysian Fields.

Jason never recovered from his experiences. Having forfeited the favour of the gods when breaking faith with Medea, he traveled as a pariah from city to city. In old age he returned to Corinth and sat under the shadow of the remains of his faithful *Argo*, remembering his past glories and lamenting his downfall. He resolved to hang himself from the prow but, before he could do so, a rotten timber fell off and killed him.

THE PLAY

Medea is a revenge tragedy that remains uniquely disturbing because it is so deeply subversive. Throughout the drama, at every level, Euripides undermines stereotypes and preconceptions, and manipulates our responses to the characters and their actions as deftly as Medea herself. This destabilization of expectation, combined with his close attention to gender conflict and racial "otherness" and his telling ironies and psychological insights, come together to make a play that shocked contemporary audiences and still feels shocking today.

Athens in the fifth century BC was at the zenith of its influence and considered itself the exemplary democracy. The virtues Athenians most admired were moral integrity, justice and hospitality, and they valued lives lived according to those precepts: without excess, in an ordered, well-proportioned way. In this patriarchal society, women had long been placed in a marginalized and subservient role; they could take no part in politics, and had a diminished legal and social position. Athens was less concerned by the women within than by the threat of the "barbarians" without. The Greeks' long-held belief in their racial superiority had hardened during the Persian invasions of 490 and 480–79 BC, and all foreigners were regarded as dangerously uncivilized and potentially violent and disruptive.

Some popular readings of *Medea* simplify the play as a radical prefeminist critique of male attitudes and authority: a drama of gender war. While it is true that Euripides attends to this conflict in thirteen of his nineteen surviving plays, and writes with great insight and sympathy on the position and psychology of women, he is more interested in creating a complex, dynamic, multifaceted character. It is through Medea that he can expose and challenge sexual ideologies, certainly, but she also allows him to address Greek xenophobia and, much more significantly, explore the ambiguous, volatile psychology of a wronged woman and how she could arrive at a state where she decides to kill her own children. The playwright achieves this by dismantling many of the prevailing orthodoxies.

The subversion of stereotypes begins with the two central characters and percolates throughout the play, as Euripides steers us through moral collapse and emotional torment. We come to Jason through his legend: as the young, intrepid hero and civilized Greek. Through the course of the drama the husband and hero is exposed—to the undoubted discomfort of the male Athenian audience—as a calculating liar: insensitive, vain and complacent. Furthermore, the betrayal that prompts the action of the play has divine repercussions. In breaking his oath to Medea, Jason has violated a religious obligation, and the audience would understand that—apart from everything else—he has also broken his oath to the gods.

Careful not to dwell on her historical reputation as a sorceress, Euripides presents Medea as the exiled Colchian: her exoticism underlined for contemporary audiences by her "foreign" dress. She is quickly established, though, as a recognizably human figure: a resolute, devoted wife and mother, victim of broken vows, deceived and humiliated by her husband. The importance she places on loyalty, honor and status—and on the necessity for revenge when those three things have been denied her—mark Medea the outsider as almost more heroic, more "masculine" than Jason the Greek. What we are witnessing is a subtle transferral of gender roles. Jason, the failing hero, is scheming, shallow and—increasingly—passive; Medea, on the other hand, is empowered, ascendant and thoroughly active.

Much of the play's sophistication, integrity and psychological impact stem from Euripides' inspired balancing of his two main characters. Our preconceptions of Jason and Medea are consistently challenged and confounded by their behavior, and the playwright uses the Chorus and Aegeus—right-thinking Athenians all—almost as director's assistants, guiding us away from received opinions and easy moral judgments.

Both protagonists are vigorously drawn and feel utterly modern, because Euripides insists on imbuing mythic characters with mortal characteristics, presenting them as ordinary people in extraordinary situations. Their endless psychological machinations, the emotional outbursts, the shabby rhetoric, the manipulation and self-deception, all ring true and timeless because Euripides employs irony, a dimension to Greek drama that previously didn't exist. His supple ironic direction of the characters towards self-exposure allows us to see clearly the motivation behind their words. The marital friction between Jason and Medea is illuminated by this approach, and by the accuracy and depth of the characterization, giving their scenes together an uncomfortable power; some of that power deriving from our recognition that not much has changed in two and a half thousand years.

This bleak modernity is reinforced by the attention paid to Medea as an outsider: both as a woman in a patriarchal society and a "barbarian" in "civilized" Greece. She is isolated from her own native land and family and has sacrificed her lineage for Jason and his country—and lineage in fifth-century Greece was a security more sought after than any love. Doubly disadvantaged as a female and a foreigner, she has the further burden of complete dependency on her husband. When he exploits her vulnerability and abandons her for a younger woman, therefore, that betrayal announces her complete social annulment. Not only that: his impending marriage will also end her sons' lineage. By overturning, effortlessly, the racial and gender stereotypes—of the ethical Greek male and the perfidious female barbarian—Euripides crucially shifts our sympathy to Medea. By the time she announces her plan to murder her children, she has won sufficient support to undercut what might have been a reflexive revulsion. We understand that she is a loving wife and mother who has been betrayed and has suffered deeply, that she knows the gravity of the crime she is about to commit, and that her punishment of the man she has come to hate requires the destruction of those she loves most. These intricate moral and emotional ambiguities invest the terrible final scene with an unusual dramatic tension.

Infanticide is, and always has been, one of the strongest taboos. From Medea's declaration of intent to the enactment itself, our sympathies start to swing away from her. The Chorus silently moves from support to opposition, objecting not to the target of retribution—Jason—but to the pawns used to secure that revenge—the children. When Medea butchers them like sacrificial lambs, we see that with these last murders she has now eradicated Jason's past, present and future. Not only that, she denies him the chance to bury his dead sons—which would be understood by the Athenian audience as deeply shameful. In the end, though, Euripides seems to have done enough. By foregrounding Medea's suffering and Jason's ruthless expediency, and finely controlling and balancing our reactions throughout the play, he prevents us from responding to the uniquely harrowing conclusion in any straightforward way. Medea may have committed an ethically repugnant crime and apparently escaped unpunished, but we have seen that she recognizes the wickedness of the act and fights against it, and it is clear that this is a hollow revenge—because it is, in a way, an act of self-destruction. At the same time, her behavior has the explicit sanction of the gods—as Jason's oath-breaking is finally punished—the chariot of Helios being the very vehicle of divine justice.

The two protagonists face each other across the stage in the last scene: alone, deracinated, empty-handed. Medea, still charged with the adrenaline of revenge, is exhausted by slaughter, on her way into exile; Jason, stripped of all hope and all artifice, is a character almost reformed by bereavement. Whatever complex emotions we feel at the end of the play, we retain just enough residual sympathy for Medea not to accept completely Jason's description of her as a dehumanized monster—because we have witnessed her grief and fury and, with that, her humanity.

NOTE ON THE TEXT

There are no manuscripts in the hand of Euripides or, indeed, any of the classical authors: the only complete transcriptions that survive are from the tenth century, and they are copies of copies. Over the centuries there have been ample opportunities for textual corruption, and texts of the play more academic than this one offer solutions of reconstruction "by conjecture." They also address the problem of interpolation, where new matter appears to have been added to expand or elaborate the original. I have used the Loeb Classical Library edition, translated and edited by David Kovacs, as my primary source, and have consulted a number of other excellent English translations—primarily those by John Davie, Alistair Elliot, James Morwood and Philip Vellacott. My main concern has been to provide an English version that is as true to the Greek as it is to the way English is spoken now.

The line numbers in this edition refer to the Greek text.

MEDEA

CHARACTERS

NURSE

TUTOR *to Medea's sons*

MEDEA

CHORUS *of Corinthian women*

CREON, *king of Corinth*

JASON

AEGEUS, *king of Athens*

MESSENGER

MEDEA'S TWO CHILDREN

Outside the house of Jason and Medea in Corinth.

Enter Nurse from the house.

NURSE

    If only it had never happened like this.
    If the *Argo* hadn't opened its sails and flown
    to Colchis through the Clashing Rocks.
    If the pines were still standing
    in the glens of Mount Pelion,
    not cut and turned
    to oars for the Argonauts.
    If Pelias the king hadn't sent those heroes
    off to do his bidding, to cross the sea
    and steal the Golden Fleece.
    It would all be different. Not as it is.
    My dear mistress, Medea,
    would never have met their leader, Jason;
    never fallen for him, head over heels,
    never left a life behind to sail away with him.
    Not tricked Pelias's daughters into killing
    their own father. And not fled here, at last,
    to Corinth, far from family and home.   10

In the beginning everything was fine.
Though a foreigner like me, Medea was welcomed
with her husband and her children—
and was happy in her new life, obedient
to Jason in everything he said and did.
In marriage that's the safest way, I think,
to follow your husband, and accept his rules.

But now this house is full of hate;
its timbers are rotten with it. Jason has gone
from her and the children, leaving them
for a royal bed. He's marrying this young thing,
the princess, daughter of Creon, the Corinthian king.
My poor Medea—dishonored—reminds him   20
of his oaths, invokes the gods of justice
and truth to witness what he's done, after all
she's done for him. To no avail.
Since she heard of his deceit
she's refused all food, and comfort;
she stays in her room and cries the days away,
won't lift her head for anyone,
won't raise her eyes from the ground.
Unmoved by words, by anything around her,
she's deaf as a stone or a wave in the sea.
Sometimes she turns to look away,   30
to call out for her father, her country
and her home: all abandoned
and betrayed for a man who now abandons her,
betrays her honor and her love.

She has learned the hard way
what it is to be an exile,
to have given up everything.

She loathes to have her children near,
and cannot bear to look at them. I am afraid
some plan is already forming in her mind.
She has a temper on her that is vile, and violent,
and she will never rest.
I know her well enough to be sure.
I fear she will creep into the palace,
stand at that double bed,
and drive a deep blade into each of them.   40
She is deadly, let me tell you,
and none who spark her rage will walk away.

Enter Tutor, escorting the two sons of Jason and Medea.

But look, here they are now, her boys,
hot from their games. They don't understand
their mother's grief; why should they?
Their minds are still too young for pain.

TUTOR

Old nurse, what are you doing,
standing out here talking to yourself?   50
Why aren't you with your mistress?

NURSE

> Old teacher, tired slave to Jason's children,
> don't you know that if the dice fall badly
> for our masters they fall the same for us?
> I feel Medea's troubles as my own,
> and have come out here
> to share them with the earth and air.

TUTOR

> So she is still crying?

NURSE

> Still crying? I envy your innocence.   60
> This is only the start.
> Her grief has just begun.

TUTOR

> The poor ignorant woman—if a servant may speak so
> of a lady. She doesn't know the news.

NURSE

> What news, old man? Don't keep it to yourself.

TUTOR

> Nothing. I shouldn't have said . . .

NURSE

> Please, I beg you as a fellow servant.
> I can keep a secret if I must.

TUTOR

Well, I was down by the sacred spring at Peirene
where the old men play at draughts
and I happened to hear something
– though I was pretending not to listen—
something about King Creon banishing these children,
and their mother, from Corinth.   70
I don't know if it's true. I hope not.

NURSE

Jason would never let that happen.
His quarrel is with Medea, not with them.

TUTOR

Old loves are dropped when new ones come along.
Jason's love no longer lives here.

NURSE

We are done for, then.
We were weathering a squall and now it turns to storm.

TUTOR

You must say nothing to your mistress,   80
this is not the time.

NURSE

Sweet children, do you hear
what kind of man your father is? He is my master,

so I cannot curse him, but such disloyalty
to those he ought to love . . . He is guilty . . .

TUTOR

What mortal man is not *guilty*?
A new woman in the bed
leaves no room for anyone else.
He has forgotten everything,
including his boys.
Has it just dawned on you
that we're each of us human:
we put ourselves above all others.

NURSE

Go into the house, children, everything will be fine.

To Tutor.

And you—keep them as far away from their mother   90
as you can; she's distraught. I've seen the way
she looks at them, like a wild animal. I'm afraid
she might do something.
She will not let this anger cool
until she's brought it down on the head of an enemy.
And I pray it is an enemy she turns on,
not those she loves . . .

MEDEA (*within*)

    Oh gods, I am so wretched, so miserable.
    Please, let me die!

NURSE

    Just as I said, children, your mother's heart's upset;
    she's stirring the pot of her darkest temper.   100
    Quickly, into the house, and don't go near her –
    don't let her see you. She is fierce, my dears,
    fierce with hate. Quick, inside!

Exit Tutor and children into the house.

    The storm is upon us.
    There is greater passion to come: lightning flashes
    to burst these black clouds of grief
    and bring down hellish weather.
    What will she do, this proud unbiddable woman,
    under the sting of this lash?   110

MEDEA (*within*)

    Do I not suffer? Have I not been wronged?
    Can I not weep? Damned children of a damned mother,
    I hope you die with your father,
    and his whole house falls around you all!

NURSE

    Oh gods! What part have they in their father's guilt?

Why do you hate *them*? Poor children,
I'm so frightened you might come to harm.

She explains to the children.

Royal minds are different to ours, and dangerous.
Being used to giving orders rather than taking them,   120
they can become outraged—and that rage is slow to cool.
Ordinary life is much better—where everyone's equal.
I hope to grow old just as I am:
lowly, unremarkable and safe.
Moderation is a lovely word and we should live by it;
it's good for our souls.
Excessiveness brings mortals no advantage. All it does
is draw more ruin on us when the gods are wild.   130

Enter a group of Corinthian women as Chorus.

CHORUS
We have heard the cry of the unhappy woman of Colchis.
Tell us, nurse. Is she still no calmer?
Even through the double doors of the inner room
we could hear her keening. It hurts our heart
to hear such sounds of sorrow
from within a house of friends.

NURSE
This house is dead. It is no longer a home.
The husband rolls in a royal bed, while the wife,   140

my mistress, stays in her room,
beyond the soothing words of any friend,
wasting her life away.

MEDEA (*within*)

Oh, let a flash of lightning pierce this skull!
What use is there in living?
Give me the freedom of death,
so I can leave behind this life I hate.

CHORUS

Did you hear that, Zeus? Sun and Earth,
did you hear that creature's dreadful cry?   150
You are rash, woman: it is just as wrong
for you to desire the bed of death as it is
for Jason to thresh in his bed of desire.
Why hurry death?
The marriage is over. Let it rest.
Let Zeus advance your cause, and save your heart.

MEDEA (*within*)

Oh mighty Themis, vengeful Artemis,   160
look down on my suffering
and these broken marriage bonds, the oaths
that bound me to my husband now all forgotten.
I will see him and his bright young bride
ground down to nothing,
and their whole house with them.
Was it for this I fled my native country, Father,

leaving you in my wake
fishing up pieces of my broken brother?

NURSE

You hear? She calls on the gods, on Themis,
daughter of Zeus, goddess of Justice   170
and guardian of all promises made by men.
Such anger is not easily appeased.

CHORUS

We wish she would come out and listen to us,
meet us face to face.
She might feel her fury lessen amongst friends.
Fetch her from the house, nurse,
and tell her we support her—   180
but be quick, before she hurts those inside.
Her passion grows so strong the air around her burns.

NURSE

I'll try, of course, but I doubt I'll persuade her.
When any of us approach
you can see her hackles rise—like a lioness
when you get between her and her cubs.
If only we could charm her with music;
but those old composers were such fools: 190
they wrote melodies only for the happy times—
festivals, grand banquets, celebrations.
None of them thought to make a music for real life,
music that would salve our wounds   200

and soothe our bitter griefs. Didn't they see
these wounds and griefs destroy us,
and a music that healed such sorrow
would be precious?
What is the point of music and song at a feast?
People are happy when they're full.
We need a tune when there's no food there to eat.

Exit Nurse into the house.

CHORUS

We hear her weeping, her litany of accusations
against her husband, the betrayer of her bed.
She calls again to Themis, goddess of oaths,
who brought her here to Greece   210
over the dark saltwater of the Black Sea,
to the locks and keys of the Hellespont,
a threshold few may cross.

Enter Medea and the Nurse from the house.

MEDEA

Women of Corinth, I have come out here
to show you who I am.
I will not be judged—by anyone—as proud.
I know many who are vain, it's true, indoors or out;
but there are others that hide themselves away,
and then people say they emulate the gods.
Whether you go out in public, or retire in private,

you get a reputation either way.
There is no justice in the eyes of men,   220
they judge by what they see, not what they know.
It is hardest for foreigners like me to be accepted
—always working, always trying to fit in—
so I have no time for those who think themselves
above the rules, or better than the others.

This blow, when it came, came from nowhere,
knocking me down,
crushing my faith in all that's good and kind.
I am lost, and foundering. The joy
has gone from my life,
and I see no reason, now, to carry on.
My husband, my companion, the man
I thought I knew so well—in whom I'd invested
everything—has revealed himself to be
the most contemptible of men.

Of all living, sentient creatures,   230
women are the most unfortunate.
We must save and save to raise a dowry;
then the man that agrees to marry us
becomes master of our bodies:
a second burden greater than the first.
Loss and insult: that is all we have.
Everything hangs on his character:
is the master good or bad?
We can refuse him nothing, but if we divorce

we are seen as somehow soiled, as damaged goods.
Innocents and strangers, we enter our husbands' houses,
with all these new laws and customs to deal with;
we need to use our intuition to teach us   240
how best to please our man.
If we do well in all our duties, and don't let him
ever think he's trapped in the marriage,
everything's fine. If not, it's death in life.

When a man's bored with what he has at home
he goes elsewhere: finds someone else to amuse him.
The woman must wait, for she is allowed
to look at one face only: his.
Men tell us that we are lucky to live safe at home
while they take up their spears and go to war.
Well, that's a lie. I'd sooner stand behind a shield   250
three times in battle than give birth once.

But yours is a different story. This is your city.
Your fathers are here;
you have the pleasures of life,
the company of friends.
I am alone in Corinth, an outsider
in a strange city far from my family—
my only company a husband
who took me as plunder from some foreign campaign
and now dishonors me. I have no mother, no brother,
no kin to turn to, to shelter me from shame.
So I shall ask this one favor from you.

If I can think of any way, any plan,   260
to make my husband pay for all this hurt,
will you keep my secret?
A woman is too timid, too weak, they say, for war
—would faint at the sight of battle-steel—
but when she is injured in love,
when her bed has been defiled, she'll have your blood.

CHORUS

We promise. You have every right
to punish your husband, Medea,
and every reason to grieve.

Enter Creon.

But here is Creon, the king.   270
Here, perhaps, with some proclamation.

CREON

So, Medea, sour-faced, glowering with rage
against your husband: hear this.
I order you now to leave this land and go into exile,
with immediate effect. Take your children with you.
I make the law and execute it, and will stay
until I've seen you off Corinthian soil.

MEDEA

No! This is the end of everything.
Fleets of enemies sail against me;

I see only rocks and no safe haven.
After so much abuse, one question, Creon: 280
why are you sending me away?

CREON

I'm afraid of you, to put it bluntly;
afraid that you will do some harm to my daughter.
I have many reasons, and they all add up.
You are a clever woman. It's known that you are skilled
in evil arts. You are wounded,
smarting at the loss of your husband from your bed.
And now I hear that you've been making threats
against the bride, her father, and the man she is to marry.
I will let nothing happen, and so will guard against it.
It's better to harden my heart against you now   290
than have you break it later.

MEDEA

My reputation, yet again! It goes before me like a curse.
My father should never have allowed me an education,
never raised me to be intelligent.
Those who are out of the ordinary
attract jealousy and bitterness.
If you try to bring new wisdom to fools,
the fools are furious;
if your mind matches the minds   300
of the city's intellectuals
then they're threatened.
But you, Creon, you are afraid.

Why is that?
What damage can I do?
I am no insurrectionist,
no insurgent against the state.
You've done nothing to me;
only given your daughter's hand away in marriage.
It's my husband I hate.   310
You've acted with propriety and good sense,
within the law, and I don't resent your happiness.
Make the marriage; I wish all of you good luck.
But let me stay. Although I have been wronged,
I will keep my peace. I yield to you as king.
You have won and I have lost.

CREON

Conciliatory words, indeed.
But still I dread to think what evil cooks within your heart.
The softness of these words makes me trust them less.
A hot-tempered woman—or man, for that matter—
is easier to stand against
than a clever one that keeps her own counsel.   320
No, I am decided.
You are hereby banished, and must leave now.
No more delay, and no more speeches.
I know you are our enemy
and I will have no enemy in our midst.

Medea kneels before him.

MEDEA

I beg you, in the name of your promised daughter.

CREON

Your words are wasted. You will never win me over.

MEDEA

You would banish me without listening to my pleas?

CREON

Yes, my family and my house mean more to me than you.

MEDEA

My country! How much I miss you now!

CREON

After my children my country is my greatest love.

MEDEA

And what a curse love is, to mortals.   330

CREON

That depends on the circumstances.

MEDEA

Zeus, do not forget who causes this suffering!

CREON

Go, foolish woman, and with you go my troubles.

MEDEA

Troubles I have in great supply.

CREON

If you don't go I'll have my soldiers throw you out.

MEDEA

No, Creon, no. I beg you . . .

CREON

You seem hell-bent on obstruction.

MEDEA

I accept my exile. I'm not asking a reprieve from that.

CREON

Why the argument then?
Why do you still cling to my hand?

MEDEA

One day. That's all I ask. Let me stay for one more day.   340
I need to think clearly where to go,
how to provide for my children—
as their father seems to have little interest.
Take pity on them, at least.
You have kindness in you; you're a parent too.
I can bear exile, but I cannot bear to see them suffer.

CREON

    It is not in my nature to be a tyrant.

    I've been merciful before, it's true, and paid the price.

    I know, even now, that I might be making a mistake,   350

    but . . . very well, you shall have your request.

    But I warn you, woman, if tomorrow's sun

    sees you and your children still within these lands, you die.

    I give you my word. One more day, if you must.

    One more is surely not enough to bring us harm.

Exit Creon. Medea rises to her feet.

CHORUS

    Unhappy woman. Where will you turn

    in this world of troubles? What protector will you find,

    what refuge? What house, what country,   360

    will save you from calamity?

    A god has abandoned you, Medea,

    in an open boat on a sea that has no shore.

MEDEA

    Evil on every side, who can deny it?

    But things are not quite as you describe.

    There are still dangers for this bride and groom,

    and for the happy father. Do you think

    I would have fawned at his knees

    without some hope of gain, without a scheme?

    I wouldn't have spoken to him,   370

    wouldn't have touched him.

But he has stumbled deep in folly now.
He had the chance to banish me, and ruin everything;
instead, he's given me this whole long beautiful day,
and time to turn all three, all three enemies
—the father, the daughter, and my husband—
into corpse-meat.

So many paths of death for them, so many choices:
I can't decide which one to take.
Shall I turn the bridal house to cinders?
Stick them all like suckling pigs?
Slink in quietly and slice them in their beds?   380
But that's the thing: if I'm caught
halfway through the plan, going in,
I will be killed and *they'll* be doing the gloating.
The best road is the most direct, a way
in which we are most skilled:
I'll take them by poison.

So be it. Now, suppose that's done.
What city will have me? What host
will offer me asylum and a safe house?
No one, at the moment. And so I'll wait.
If some place of refuge suddenly appears,   390
then I can proceed by stealth;
if time or circumstance force me into the open
I will use the sword—though I am sure to die for it—
and drive it into them with my own brave hand.
By the goddess Hecate, whom I worship above all,

none of them will live to laugh at me. I'll turn
their marriage and this family alliance airless and black,
and blacken the day they chose to banish me.   400
Come, Medea, use all your dark skills and do your worst!
This is now a contest of courage.
Do you see what's being done to you?
Trying to marry Jason to some relative of Sisyphus
the oath-breaker, when he had *you* as a wife—you,
granddaughter to Helios, god of the sun!
You know what you must do.

She turns to the Chorus.

And being women,
barred by birth from the noble deeds of men,
we have mastered the art of manipulation—
to become the most skillful architects of harm.

CHORUS

The sacred river-water flows uphill. The laws of nature,   410
and of humans, all reversed.
Now we see men dissemble, twist their words
and break their holy vows, so it must follow soon
that women will have rights, that women
—not men—are the ones we hold in high repute.
No more gossip and rumor to keep us in check;   420
the natural order has turned around.

The old songs will have to change.
No more hymns to our faithlessness and deceit.
Apollo, god of song, lord of the lyre,
never passed on the flame of poetry to us.
But if we had that voice, what songs
we'd sing of men's failings, and their blame.
History is made by women, just as much as men.   430

We'd sing of how you sailed to this land, Medea,
from your father's house: love-driven,
through the twin rocks of the eastern sea.
You were a stranger,
and you're now estranged again—
losing your husband's love, your husband's bed,
your home, and now the right to stay.

Promises and oaths mean nothing here,
are nothing more than smoke. There is no honor, now,
in all of Greece—and, in dishonor, little shame.   440
You have no family home, no shelter,
and a young princess holds your husband in thrall—
and in your house holds sway.

Enter Jason.

JASON

This is not the first time I've seen this savage temper,
but I hope it will be the last.
You are impossible to deal with.

You could have stayed here, kept your home,
if you had only agreed
to the arrangements of your superiors.
A small price to pay, I would have thought, but no.
You have been exiled for your foolish talk,   450
and it's your own fault. You can call me what you like
and I don't mind, but to rant against the king?
You're lucky it's just exile; you're lucky to be alive.
I tried to calm him, as I wanted you to stay,
but you wouldn't hold your tongue, would you?
Your slander and curses have seen you banished.

However, in spite of this, I will not fail my loved ones.
I come here, woman, still thinking about your interests.   460
You and the children will not go into exile
penniless or in need of anything.
Banishment brings many hardships, I imagine.
I want you to know that whatever hatred you feel for me,
I could never bear you any malice.

MEDEA

There are no names for something
as foul and spineless as you.
A man who is no man at all.
How dare you come to us here,
where you are most despised.
Is this your idea of courage or heroism,   470
to wrong your family and then *visit* them?
Loathsome, shameless, evil man.

But part of me is glad you're here:
it will ease my heart a little
to spear you with my words and see you squirm.

Let's start at the beginning.
I saved your life—as every Greek on the *Argo* will confirm.
I helped you harness the fire-breathing bulls,
plough the field of death, sow the dragon's teeth.   480
I killed the sleepless serpent, guardian of the Golden Fleece,
and lit you to safety. I abandoned my father and my home
and went with you to Iolcos: showing more love than sense.
I had King Pelias—who sent you on the quest—
butchered by his daughters
in the most horrible of deaths, reducing him
to a broth of bones,
turning his blood-line off.
I did this all for you. And what in return?
You drop me for some *girl*.
Even though we have children, you forget me.
I could almost understand all this—all this lust—   490
if you were childless, but we have two beautiful sons.

What do you believe in?
You lie as a matter of course;
all your promises and oaths are broken, wholesale.
Do you think the old gods no longer rule,
and you can set up new statutes
to match your moral turpitude?
You can't even keep your word to me,

your simple word, to love and cherish.
Look at this hand you took in your hands;
these knees you clung to.
All empty gestures; cheap, meaningless lies.
You are a husk of a man,
and you have cheated me of my life.

Let me share my thoughts, as if you were an old friend.   500
As if you were a friend.
Here are some questions
which might make you feel uncomfortable.
Where can I go now? Home to my father?
I betrayed him and my country by sailing off with you.
To the miserable daughters of Pelias?
How they'll welcome me, their father's murderer!
This is how things stand: I made enemies of those I loved,
for you; harmed those I had no need to harm, for you.
In return, you made me "happy"—
at least in the eyes of many Greek women: 510
"What a lucky girl, to have such a good and faithful husband!"
A husband who stands watching
as I'm sent into exile with my children,
with no allies and no place to go.
Is this your wedding gift to yourself,
to see the woman who saved you,
and the sons that she bore, banished as beggars?
O Zeus, we can tell real gold from imitation by the hallmark;
why is there no mark on men to tell the true ones from
    the false?

CHORUS

There is no anger worse than this,   520
when dearest love has turned to deepest hate.

JASON

I see I must be a skillful captain once more,
and steer carefully: I'll trim my sail
and run before the storm of all your words.
Let's get this straight.
You wildly overstate your role in all this.
It was Aphrodite who saved the *Argo*, Aphrodite alone.
You are clever enough, surely,
to see that the rest was all Eros and his arrows.   530
Not to put too fine a point on it, you were driven by Desire.
You helped me, of course you did, and I'm grateful,
but you gained more than you gave.
You are with Greeks now, not gypsies—
in a land of culture and justice, not some tribal swamp.
You are known throughout Greece for that brain of yours;
would you be famous back where you came from,   540
on the very edge of the world? I don't think so.
Personally, I can't see any use for a house of gold
or an Orphic voice if there's no one to see it,
and no one to hear. We build our lives on accolades,
and Greece, I have to say, is the very cradle of fame.

Well, enough about what you did for me
on the "Labors of Jason";
anyway, you're the one who brought it up.

As to my marriage, my *royal* marriage,
I will show you just how wise and prudent I have been,
and what a great friend I am to you and the children . . . 550

Medea makes a gesture of impatience.

No! Hold your tongue and listen!
When I moved here from Iolcos,
dragging bad luck behind me,
what better good fortune could I find
than marriage to the daughter of a king?
And I, an exile! I know you think I'm tired of you,
and lust for younger flesh,
that I want to rival others who have many children.
Not true: I have enough children.
My one motive was to ensure security, and prosperity. 560
I don't want to end up as some vagrant
men cross the street to avoid.
I want to raise the children
in a manner befitting my position;
perhaps there might be other children, later on
—royal brothers for our sons—
and so our blood-lines join.
And with that: security for all.
You don't need more children, surely.
But *royal* sons: now, *that's* useful—
and they'd be great companions
for the ones we already have.
Is that such a bad ambition?

If it weren't for this sexual jealousy, you'd agree.
You women are all the same. If you're happy in bed   570
then you're happy everywhere; but if that goes wrong
then the world might as well be over,
and you turn on those closest to you.
If we could produce children some other way,
without the need of women, then—believe me—
all human misery would end.

CHORUS

Jason, your argument is impressive, and eloquently put.
However, if you'll pardon us, we don't see
that deserting your wife is morally right.

MEDEA

Well, Jason, that's one way of looking at it.
I see things from a different point of view.
An eloquent brute is still a brute.   580
Someone who defends their evil plausibly
deserves the greatest punishment.
And that goes for you.
You cannot dazzle me with gilded words and fancy rhetoric,
nor can a thousand pretty phrases cover up your crime.
Your arrogance is matched only by your stupidity.
If I pull one thread, the whole thing unravels.
If this marriage is so sensible you could have been honest
and talked it through with me first, won me over.
But no, you kept your grubby secret to yourself.
Have you *ever* told the truth?

JASON

> I can just imagine what a great support you'd have been
> if I'd mentioned the marriage. Look at you:
> you can barely control your bestial rage as it is.   590

MEDEA

> That wasn't really what stopped you from speaking, was it?
> I think it was simply this: you're getting old,
> your deeds of heroism are barely remembered,
> and you're still saddled with a foreigner for a wife.

JASON

> Believe me: this is not about "another woman."
> This royal marriage, as I've said before,
> was for you and the children.
> The boys would have princes for brothers,
> and everyone would be safe.

MEDEA

> What perilous safety! I pray I never reach it—
> or find this prosperity that would empty my heart.

JASON

> Pray for something wiser. Pray instead   600
> for a less pessimistic view of life:
> not to find pain in what is pleasant;
> not to feel unlucky when you're not.

MEDEA

Not unlucky? I go friendless into exile,
while you sit in the royal palace—
you tell me I'm *fortunate*?

JASON

You brought this on yourself.
You have no one else to blame.

MEDEA

What did I do? Did *I* take a wife and abandon *you*?

JASON

You cursed the king, and the royal house.

MEDEA

Yes, and I will be a curse to your house too.

JASON

This is pointless. If I can help with some money   610
towards your . . . for the future, for the children and yourself,
just say. I'm prepared to be generous,
and I'm happy to give you letters to bring to friends abroad,
who'll take you in, I'm sure. Look, this is a good offer;
why don't you just swallow your pride,
and your anger, and accept it?

MEDEA

I need no friends of yours to take me in.
And I'll have nothing to do with your money either.
Is that for "compensation" or just to shut me up?
The gifts of the damned are poison.

JASON

Well, let the gods be my witness:
I have done everything I can.
I've offered to help you and the children   620
but my kindness is thrown back in my face.
Such obstinacy will only make things worse for you.

MEDEA

Go. Get out of my sight.
I can tell you're keen to get back to the palace
and your hot little playmate. She'll be waiting in bed,
I imagine, dying for it.
Go, play the bridegroom while you can,
because I tell you this:
your honeymoon will be brief, and bitter as gall.

Exit Jason.

CHORUS

When it comes over us too strongly,
Desire destroys our sense and wrecks our reputation,
but, if she comes in gently,
no one brings such happiness as Aphrodite.   630

We beg you, goddess, do not bend your golden bow
and loose your arrows against us.
They never miss, we know, and they are tipped with lust.

Let restraint and chastity be our watchwords:
the best gifts of the gods. Aphrodite would drive us,
ravenous, from chamber to chamber, inflaming passions
of the head and heart, leaving us open, unconcealed.   640
We pray that she chooses wisely who we wed,
or every bed is turned into a battlefield.

Dear country, dear home, may we never
be driven away from you, never drift through life—
given pity, but not the help we need.
We'd rather bring life's daylight to an end
than be banished—to see all corners of the world   650
but never see our native land again.

We've witnessed it ourselves, not just heard the stories:
no city will accept you, no friend
will remember your past kindnesses and take you in.
Those who cannot honor friends will die unloved.   660
Let hearts and doors be left unlocked, we pray,
leave them open for the lost.

Enter Aegeus.

AEGEUS
　　Medea, blessings: I know no better greeting for a friend.

MEDEA

And blessings to you as well, Aegeus, son of wise Pandion.
What brings the king of Athens here, to Corinth?

AEGEUS

I've been to the ancient oracle of Apollo.

MEDEA

To Delphi, the very center of the world! What took you
there?

AEGEUS

To ask for the strength to father children.

MEDEA

You've lived so long a life and never had a child? 670

AEGEUS

I have no heir; some god blocks me.

MEDEA

But you have a wife . . .

AEGEUS

Yes. I have a wife.

MEDEA

What did Apollo say?

AEGEUS

A complicated riddle.

MEDEA

May I hear it?

AEGEUS

Of course. Your cleverness may crack its code.

MEDEA

Then tell me.

AEGEUS

I was told, "Do not untie the wineskin's neck . . ."

MEDEA

Till when? Till you go where?   680

AEGEUS

". . . Until you return to your native land."

MEDEA

Athens. So what brings your fleet to Corinth?

AEGEUS

I must visit Pittheus, king of Troezen.

MEDEA

Son of Pelops. A most pious man, they say.

AEGEUS

I will tell him the words of the oracle.

MEDEA

He is wise, and knows about these things.

AEGEUS

And he's an old supporter: the closest of my allies.

MEDEA

Well, I wish you luck: I hope you get what you want.

AEGEUS (*noticing Medea's distraught demeanor*)

But Medea, why the tears? What's wrong?

MEDEA

Oh Aegeus, my husband is the worst of men. 690

AEGEUS

What do you mean?

MEDEA

Jason wrongs me, though I've done no wrong to him.

AEGEUS

Why? What's happened?

MEDEA

He has taken another woman to be his wife
and mistress of his house.

AEGEUS

What! He would do something that wicked?

MEDEA

He has. I was once loved, but now I'm cast aside.

AEGEUS

Was it love or simple lust? Did he tire of you?

MEDEA

Great lust. Lust for something we cannot give him.

AEGEUS

Forget him, then, as he is clearly worthless.

MEDEA

His lust is royal: he will marry the king's daughter.   700

AEGEUS

Tell me everything. Which king?

MEDEA

Creon, king of Corinth.

AEGEUS

I see. Now I understand your distress.

MEDEA

And that's not everything. I am banished.

AEGEUS

Worse and worse. By whom?

MEDEA

The king, again.

AEGEUS

And Jason stands back and lets this happen? Shameful.

MEDEA

He stands and blusters at our exile,
but he seems to be coming to terms with it.

She kneels before Aegeus.

Aegeus, I beg you, pity me. Take pity
on a suffering friend turned out into the cold.   710
Please, take me: receive me into your country,
into your home. And in return?
This longing of yours for children:
trust me, it will be relieved.
The gods will give you the son you desire.
You'll end your life fulfilled.

41

Fate has smiled on you today, bringing us together like
   this.
I'll cure you of your childlessness, believe me.
I have many remedies for that.

AEGEUS

You warm my heart, Medea.
There are good reasons to grant you this favor.   720
To appease the gods, for one, but mostly
the promise of a son: that is not something I can do alone.
It is settled. If you reach Athens
I will try and act as your protector.
But I make this one condition:
I cannot help you in your flight from Corinth.
Once in my house, though, you'll be safe;
I'll give you up to no one.
But you must journey alone. I cannot intervene here,
amongst allies, and offend my hosts.   730

MEDEA

Of course.
If you would give me your word on this, I will have all I wish.

AEGEUS

Don't you trust me? What is troubling you?

MEDEA

You, I trust.
But the house of Pelias, on the other hand,

is hostile, and that of Creon.
If you are bound by an oath
I know you won't hand me over to my enemies.
Words are one thing,
but words are open to manipulation—diplomacy . . .
An oath sworn by the gods is inviolable.
I am weak; I need that strength against their royal power.   740

AEGEUS

You are shrewd, Medea, and I'm happy to agree.
It suits me, too, as my security—and a good excuse
for me to give to your enemies, to argue your case.
Name the gods I must swear by.

MEDEA

Swear by the soil of the Earth,
by Helios, my grandfather, god of the sun,
then by the whole pantheon.

AEGEUS

You must tell me what I swear to do, or not to do.

MEDEA

That you will never expel me from Athens,
and never deliver me to my enemies,   750
as long as you may live.

AEGEUS

    I swear by Earth, by the holy light of Helios,
    and by all the gods, that I will do as you say.

MEDEA (*rises to her feet*)

    Perfect.
    And if you don't abide by this oath, what punishment?

AEGEUS

    May I be damned: the fate of all who scorn the gods.

MEDEA

    Go in happiness and peace. All is now well.
    I shall come to your city as soon as I can—
    once I have finished here. I have a few things left to do.

    *Exit Aegeus as the Chorus gives the travel-blessing. Nurse appears
       at door of palace.*

CHORUS

    May Hermes, Maia's son, guide of travelers,
    bring you safely home, my lord,   760
    and may whatever you desire be yours, Aegeus,
    for you are a generous man.

MEDEA

    Oh Zeus! Justice of Zeus! Light of Helios!
    Now I sense victory. I have my enemies in my sight,
    my sails are set and the winds are with me.

Just when everything seemed hopeless, storm-tossed,
this man appears and offers me safe harbor.
I will lash fast to his mooring-place   770
when I am done with Corinth.

And now I'll tell you my plan—
which will give you little pleasure.
I will send a servant to Jason to request a visit.
When he arrives, I'll ply him with soft words:
"I've changed my mind," I'll say, "you're right;
it's quite the best decision to let us go,
and make a royal marriage; such wisdom,
and in all our interests. One favor only:
let the children stay."   780
Not that I would ever leave them here to this rabble,
no—they will be my messengers of death.
I'll send them to the princess, bearing gifts:
a finely woven gown of silk and a diadem of beaten gold.
But in this finery I will smear the fatal oil,
so when she puts it on she'll put on poison.
She will die in agony, as will anyone who touches her.

That much is easy,   790
but what comes next I can hardly bear to say.
I shall kill the children. My children.
No one will ever take them from me.
Then, once the house of Jason lies in ruin,
I'll escape from Corinth, fleeing
the murder of my own dear sons:

that most unutterable of crimes.
I will not endure the scorn of enemies. 800
So let it begin. There is nothing left for me to lose.
I should never have fled my father's house,
falling for the words of a Greek.
But, with the help of the gods, he will pay such a price.
He will never see the sons he had by me alive again—
nor will he see children from his new bride.
He'll just see her: writhing and dying from my poisons.
Let no man say of Medea that she is mild as milk;
I am not like other women: I am of some other kind.
I love my own—and will destroy
all those who stand against me.
I was born for a life of the greatest glory. 810

CHORUS

You've made us listen; made us party to your plan.
We must remind you of humanity's simple laws.
You must not do this dreadful thing.

MEDEA

There is no other way.
I forgive you, though, for your words.
This is my suffering, not yours.

CHORUS

But woman, how can you bear to kill your own children?

MEDEA

It is the way to hurt him most.

CHORUS

And bring you the deepest misery.

MEDEA

Be that as it may. Enough:
we have passed the time for talking.

To Nurse.

You: go and fetch Jason.   820
I choose you because I trust you.
Tell him nothing of my plans.
Be loyal to me as your mistress, and as a fellow woman.

Exit Nurse.

CHORUS

Athens: unravaged, unconquered and unspoilt.
Your people—sons and daughters of Erechtheus—
have flourished in your holy land since ancient times.
Blessed by the gods, they grow from your fertile soil,
nurtured by art and wisdom, moving graceful through   830
the same clear air as the nine Pierian Muses moved
when they were born to Harmonia, the golden-haired.

They say that Aphrodite dipped her cup
in the sweet stream of the Cephisus,
blowing gentle breezes down across the land.   840
A garland of fragrant roses in her hair,
she taught Eros to sit and learn at Wisdom's side,
learning to work for grace and excellence and art.

So how then will this city of sacred streams,
home of hospitality, accept you now?
How could it let a child-killer, hands still caked in blood,   850
walk among its gentle citizens?
Consider what you're about to do:
their young bodies and the terrible wounds.
We beg you: think again. Do not hurt your sons!

How will you find it in yourself? How will you dare?
How will you blind the eye and blacken the heart
enough to drive a blade into the flesh you love?   860
When they look up at you, their mother,
with her arm raised, will you be butcher enough
to spray the walls with blood?

Enter Jason accompanied by the Nurse.

JASON

I have come, as you asked.
Despite your hatred, I'm still here.
What do you want from me now?

MEDEA

Jason, I want to beg your forgiveness for what I said before.
You know my wild temper, you've put up with it   870
during our many happy years of love.
I've thought this through and think I've been a fool.
"Obstinate, stupid woman," I've told myself,
"why do you rant and rave in the face of sound advice?
Why make yourself an enemy to the king
and to your husband, who thinks only of what's best for us,
marrying the princess so our children can have brothers?"
I say to myself, "Can you never control your rage?
What's the matter with you? The gods have been so kind,   880
and provide so well for everything you need.
Do you not have the children? Have you forgotten
you are in exile here and friends are thin on the ground?"

These are my thoughts. I realize now I was being foolish,
and angry for no reason.
So now I agree with everything you propose.
You've made a royal alliance on our behalf,
and instead of supporting you—planning the big day,
standing by the marriage bed, tending to your young bride—
I've been selfish, and stupid, and weak.
But I am a woman. I'm not saying we're wicked by nature:
we are what we are. Not wicked, perhaps, but foolish.   890
But you shouldn't lower yourself
and match my foolishness with your own.
That's in the past, though. I admit that I was wrong.
I am wiser now, and will behave more prudently.

Children, children! Come outside!

The children enter with the Tutor.

Say hello to your father, come and talk to him.
Let's leave all the cross words behind. We're friends now
and no one's angry any more. Take his hand in yours.
Ah, the pain of it! The pain of what I know the future
    holds   900
and I must hide. Oh, children!
Will you stretch out your little arms like this forever?
It breaks my heart.
Oh, what a fool I am to weep so easily.
Here am I, finally making up with your father,
and all I do is cry.

CHORUS
    Fresh tears start from our eyes as well.
    Pray to the gods this evil goes no further!

JASON
    This is much better, woman, I approve of this.
    I don't blame you for your earlier mood;
    it's only natural for a woman to get angry when a
        husband   910
    brings another marriage into the house.
    But now you understand the logic of it, finally,
    and recognize the brilliance of the plan.
    I'm impressed by your maturity.

And you, my sons:
your father has given much thought to your future
and, I'm happy to say that—with the gods' help—
arrangements are in place to provide for you.
Some day, you and your new brothers
will be the top men of Corinth.
But first you must grow up, big and strong.   920
Leave all the rest to your father—and the kindly gods.
I can't wait to see you tall and proud in your manhood,
ready to trample my enemies!

Medea turns away weeping.

What now, woman? *More* tears?
Why are you crying instead of being pleased at what I say?

MEDEA

It's nothing. I was thinking of the children.

JASON

But why, for heaven's sake, are you upset about the children?

MEDEA

I am their mother, Jason.   930
When you talked of them as men
it made me wonder if they'd get that far,
and sad to think of it.
They are so little, and life is so hard.

JASON

    I've taken care of everything. Don't you worry.

MEDEA

    If you say so. It's not that I distrust your words,
    it's just that we women are soft by nature and quick to tears.

    But you came so we could talk.
    I've said some of what I meant to say, but here's the rest.
    Creon has resolved to exile me from Corinth
    and I understand, it's for the best.
    I have no wish to stand in the way of him, or you,
    and those who think I hate the royal family.
    So, I will go into exile.
    But the children deserve a better life than mine.
    Let them stay and be raised here in your house,
    that's all I ask. For their sake, make this plea to Creon.   940

JASON

    I'm not sure I will persuade him, but I'll try . . .

MEDEA

    Ask your—ask the princess to plead the case,
    that they not be sent away.

JASON

    Very well. I think I can do that;
    I'm sure she can win him over.

MEDEA

If she's a woman like all other women. But let me help.
I'll send her presents, the most beautiful things,
and the boys can deliver them.
One of you servants, quickly,   950
fetch the silk dress and the golden coronet!

One of the servants goes into the house.

To Jason.

She will have not just *one* happiness, but many.
A hero for a husband and also these:
passed down from Helios, my grandfather, to me—
these treasures of the sun.

The servant returns with the gifts.

Boys, take these presents.
You must give them to the princess yourselves,
into her royal hands. They are gifts that will fit her perfectly.

JASON

Why are you giving away your finest things?
Do you think the royal palace is short of silk and gold?   960
Don't just hand over heirlooms as rich as these;
keep them for yourself! If I know my bride
she'll value my wishes over any of your gifts,
however pretty. Trust me on this.

MEDEA
I won't hear another word.
Even the gods are swayed by tributes;
and as for mortals, gold outweighs ten thousand words.
The day is hers, and hers is the brightest star.
She's young, and royal, and shortly to be heaven-blessed.
And anyway, to save my sons from exile
I'd barter with my soul, not just a crown of gold.

Now, children, take these presents to the palace,
and carry them carefully to the princess, the happy bride,   970
my mistress now, and ask her—beg her—
not to have you sent away. Give her the gifts,
and make sure she takes them in her own hands.
Go quickly now, and come back soon,
and bring the news your mother longs to hear!

Exit Jason and children, accompanied by the Tutor and the Nurse.

CHORUS
There's no hope for those children now, not any more.
Already they are walking on the road to death.
Seeing the gold, the bride will welcome them,
accept the presents, then hold catastrophe in her hands.
And with those hands she'll raise the coronet
to her blonde head, and on that head set   980
vanity, the bright blazonry of death.

How could she resist such gleaming beauty?
She will put on the gown, and the wreath
of wrought gold, to dress herself for the bridal bed,
crowned for a royal wedding.
But she has dressed herself for the grave,
her new and final home.
There's no escape:
the snare is tightening as we speak these words.

And you, Jason, marrying into the house of kings   990
—or so you think—you bring destruction to your children,
and agony to your bride. How wrong you were
about your destiny! How far you have wandered
from the hero's path! Reduced to this:
to be the groom of death, losing everything but your life.

And lastly you, Medea, a mother still:
so jealous of your marriage bed you'd kill your children.
All this because of another woman,   1000
your husband's treachery, his desertion too,
you'd do all this:
you'd kill the sons you carried in your womb?

Enter Tutor with the children.

TUTOR

My lady, the children are reprieved from exile!
The princess took your gifts, delighted, into her own hands.
All is well. They have no enemies in the palace.

Medea turns away and weeps.

What's wrong? Is that not good news?

MEDEA

Cruel news.

TUTOR

These words are out of tune.

MEDEA

Cruel.

TUTOR

Have I said something wrong?
I thought you would be pleased. 1010

MEDEA

You have said what you have said. It's not you I blame.

TUTOR

Then why are you staring at the ground?
Why are you weeping?

MEDEA

Old man, I have every reason. The gods,
and my own madness, have led us all to this.

TUTOR

Take heart, my lady, in time your sons
will come to bring you home.

MEDEA

I will bring home many before then. Oh gods!

TUTOR

You're not the first woman to be separated from her children.
We mortals must learn to bear misfortune.

MEDEA

I will try. Now, go inside and see to the boys.   1020
Just as you would normally.

Exit Tutor.

Children, children, you have a city now, and a home.
Leaving me to grieve, you will stay here forever.
I am going somewhere else, into exile,
and will never see you growing up—
watch your weddings, meet your wives.
What misery I've brought on myself!
It was all for nothing: the pains of labor, years of
  rearing—   1030

the worries and the fears of being a mother!
I had such hopes for you, such hopes:
that you would care for me when I grew old and,
when I died, dress me for burial with your own dear hands.
These dreams were sweet, but have come to nothing.
Without you, I'll live out my days in pain and grief.
And you will never again look on your mother
with those kind and loving eyes.
You will have gone from me.

Dear sons, why do you stare at me like that?   1040
Why do you smile these last smiles?

To Chorus.

What am I going to do? My heart gives way
when I see their shining faces. My poor babies.
I can't do it. Forget all the schemes.
I'll take them away with me, away from here.
Why should I hurt *them*, just to punish him?
When I would suffer twice as much?
I won't do it. I won't think of it again.

But wait, what's going on?
Could I leave here without seeing my enemies punished?
Leave Corinth a laughing stock?   1050
I must steel myself, and do it.
What a coward I am, to let such softness dull my blade.
Children! In, into the house!

Anyone without the stomach for sacrifice: keep well away.
My hand will not weaken now.

No! No! No! Stop this raging of the heart! Let them be,
monstrous woman, leave their young lives alone!
We could all be happy and safe in Athens . . .
No! No! No! By the furies of Hell,
I'll not abandon them to my enemies and their violation. 1060
It's all done now, anyway; there's no escape.
They must die too. And since they must,
the one who gave them life must be the one to end it.

The children begin to move towards the house.

The crown will be on her head by now,
and in her golden veil the bride lies dying.
The pace quickens. I take one road of sorrow,
and send my children on a sadder one.
I must say goodbye.

The children return to Medea.

Give me your hand to kiss, dear son; yours too.   1070
My beautiful children: my noble, beautiful children!
May you both be peaceful where you go.
Your father has taken away all chance of happiness here.
What it means to hold you! Your skin is so soft.
These little kisses; your sweet, milky breath . . . my
    babies . . . Go.

Go now. Go! I cannot even see you, through my pain.
And there is more pain yet to come.
And horror, boundless horror.
I understand what I'm about to do,
but the rage in my heart is stronger than my reason.
There, that is it. Passion is the root of all our sin,
and all our suffering.   1080

Exit children into the house.

CHORUS
On the matter of children: many times we've argued,
many times we've lost. Men's skill in rhetoric
is more subtle, more practiced than our own.
But women have a Muse, too, who gives us wisdom,   1090
and this is our opinion: those men and women
who have never brought up children are, by nature, blessed.
They never suffer those extremes.

Look at the parents, worn down by love and worry.   1100
Are their little ones sick? Are they hungry?
Will they grow up well, or badly? And worst of all,
after years of this, the fear all parents know:
that they'll outlive their children. That Death will come,
with his casual, careless hand, and knock them off the world.

Yet we persist—in search of love, or heirs,   1110
or some brief brilliant proof that we exist—
and the fruit of all this anxious love is grief.

MEDEA

My sisters, enough.

I have been waiting a long time for this.

And now it comes. At last.

A message from the palace.

Look, Jason's servant struggles for breath.

My goodness, he is choking on his news.   1120

Enter servant of Jason as Messenger.

MESSENGER

Medea, what you've done is unspeakable.

Beyond all human laws.

You must leave this place, by any means you choose,

but you must leave now.

MEDEA

Why? What's happened?

MESSENGER

She's dead, the princess, and her father Creon too.

Both dead, by your poison.

MEDEA

Ah! Excellent news.

From this day I will count you as friend and benefactor.

MESSENGER

What? You are beyond madness, beyond decency—
to commit murder on the royal house and then *celebrate*?   1130

MEDEA

I have many reasons for *that*,
but why should I explain to you?
We come from different worlds.
Calm down. Take your time.
Don't spare the details.
I'd like to know just how they died.
The worse it was, the more I want to hear.

MESSENGER

When your two little sons came, hand in hand,
and entered the palace with their father,
there was great joy among the servants.
We'd all felt sorry for the way you'd been treated,
but now the word was out
that you and Jason had made your peace.   1140
So we were pleased to welcome the boys,
blessing their hands and heads with kisses
as they passed through to the women's quarters.
I was so happy that I followed them to the royal chamber.
The mistress—whom we honor now,
as once we honored you—had eyes only for Jason.
When she saw the boys she veiled her lovely face
and turned away, upset that they were there.
Your husband soothed her sulky mood and said: 1150

"Don't be cross with them, they're only children.
Come, look up, my dear, these boys are now your family too.
Accept these gifts with royal grace,
and ask your father to release them from this exile
for the future of our happiness, and for my sake."

Seeing the beautiful presents, she was won over,
and agreed to all that Jason asked.
Your children and their father had scarcely left the room
before she took the silken gown and put it on.   1160
Then she placed the golden crown on her head,
arranging her hair in a hand-mirror,
smiling at the stillness that she found reflected there.
Rising, she stepped elegantly
up and down the room in her bare feet,
delighted with her gifts. Every now and then she'd stop,
twisting round to admire the dress and how it fell
in perfect folds to her ankles, so young and fine and strong.

Then, suddenly, all this beauty turned to horror.
Her color changed, her legs began to shake,
and she staggered backwards,   1170
just managing to collapse into a chair.
One of the servant-women,
thinking that the frenzy of Dionysus,
or some lesser god, possessed her mistress,
raised a shout in praise—until she saw
the mouth of the princess bubbling with a white froth,
her eyes rolling back in her head,

her body draining of blood. That servant's call
turned to a scream, and the others scattered:
some to fetch the father, some the husband.
The whole palace rang with running feet.   1180

All this took place in a few moments,
the time it would take to cover two hundred yards,
and she just sat there, eyes closed, in a speechless trance.
Then suddenly woke, to the noise and stench of burning;
to the sound of her own shrieking.
Hers was a double agony: the golden crown
began to stream with molten flame, and the delicate gown,
gift of your sons, started eating into her clear flesh.
As fire lapped at her she leaped up from the chair and ran,
shaking her head and her long hair, this way and that,   1190
trying to throw off the blazing crown.
But the gold was welded tight and would not move,
and the more she shook her head the more the flames flew.
Till finally, exhausted by this agony, she fell to the floor—
unrecognizable to anyone, except her father.
Her eyes and face were gone:
blood and flame dropped, spitting,
from the places where they'd been.
The poisoned flesh dripped off her   1200
like resin from a pine torch.
It was a sight too gruesome to bear
and we had seen too much—and were too afraid—
to touch the smoking corpse.

But not her father, who at this moment stumbled in,
not knowing how she'd died.
Falling at her side, he threw his arms around her,
kissing her and crying, "My poor sweet angel,
what god has destroyed you in this hideous way?
Who has robbed me of my only child? And I,
so close to death? Let me die beside my daughter!"   1210
And so he lay there until his tears had stilled at last.
But as he tried to struggle to his feet, he found
he was stuck fast to the glittering gown,
like ivy clings to a laurel branch,
and a ghastly wrestling match began.
As he tried to get up on one knee, his dead daughter
in her dress would drag him down. When he used
his little strength to free himself, each tug would
tear the old flesh from his bones. Finally he
gave up, sank back, and breathed his last.
And so they now lay side by side in death,   1220
father and daughter:
a sight that would make the world weep.

To Medea.

What happens to you, Medea, I cannot say.
You will learn, soon enough, your punishment—
though you will find some way, no doubt, to evade it.
All I know is that human life is nothing but a shadow—
that those men we call most clever, crafters of words
and shapers of theories, are the greatest fools.

No mortal man is happy:
lucky, yes; prosperous perhaps, but happy, never.   1230

Exit Messenger.

CHORUS

This day the gods have turned their eyes to Jason:
sending him calamity and justice, in equal measure.

MEDEA

And so, friends, now my course is clear.
I must kill the children quickly and be gone.
Any delay delivers them to murder by some other blade.
They must die, in any case, and as they must it is I,   1240
who gave them life, must kill them. Let my heart
be armored against this awful but necessary act.
Let my luckless hand take up the sword
and walk toward the edge. Let there be no weakness now,
no tender memories of their birth, of them as babies:
forget them now, and weep for them after.
Even if they are killed, they once were loved.
Unlike me, unlucky woman that I am.   1250

Exit Medea into the house.

CHORUS

Hear us, Mother Earth! Turn your gaze, Helios,
high god of the sun, look down now
on this fiery woman before she

sinks her hands in the blood of her children.
It's not just *their* blood she spills, but hers, and yours.
She sprang from your gold seed.
It would be a god's blood on the ground,
god's blood dripping from a mortal sword.
This is transgression.
Prevent her, lords of Heaven, intercede against her!
She is a fiend and Fury in this house.
Reach down—great gods—to stay her vengeance, and her
    hand! 1260

All is waste. You became a wife, bore children,
left behind another life behind the Clashing Rocks.
All lost. Was it for this you came so far,
to let rage devour your heart and stain this land with
    murder?
With the murder of your own?
Even the gods blanch and come among us
when they see us kill our kin. 1270

CHILDREN (*within*)
    Aaah!

CHORUS
    Did you hear that? The boy's cry? She is a monster.

FIRST CHILD (*within*)
    Help! Help! Mother, let me go!

SECOND CHILD (*within*)

Don't kill us!

CHORUS

Should we go in? We could save the children's lives . . .

FIRST CHILD (*within*)

Help us, please! She has a knife!

SECOND CHILD (*within*)

No! No! Please Mother, don't! Please . . .

CHORUS

Hellish witch!
You must be made of stone or iron,   1280
to cut down your own like this!
Only one woman before you
could bring herself to commit such crimes,
and she was mad—Ino,
dispatched by Hera to wander the world.
She stepped off a cliff-edge with her boys.
She killed them *and* herself.
But Medea is not mad. And Medea survives.
What more horror can there be?
Sex leads to death, inexorably,
and grief is in the very seed of life.   1290

Enter Jason.

JASON

You women standing there—
is she inside, that vile bitch?
Or has she fled?
She'll have to hide herself under the earth,
or find wings to fly to heights beyond it,
to escape my terrible vengeance
and the royal steel of Corinth.
She has killed the king;
she has killed my bride, the princess.
Now she herself must die.   1300

But it's the boys I've come for.
I'm here to save the lives of my sons.
With so much murder in the air,
I fear that Creon's family might seek revenge,
and get at that harpy through her children—
through them: my sweet boys.

CHORUS

Jason, you have no idea how bad it really is:
much worse than anything you've said.

JASON

What could be worse?
Is Medea going to kill me too?

CHORUS

> No, but she has killed your children.
> Both your sons are dead.

JASON

> Dead? My sons?   1310
> You would make me dead as well . . .

CHORUS

> Your children are no more.

JASON

> Where? Where did she kill them? In the house? Where?

CHORUS

> Open the doors and you will find the slaughter.

JASON

> Unbolt them. Let me see this double evil:
> my boys, and their killer—the woman I will kill.

> *Jason tries to open the doors of the house. Medea appears in a*
> *winged chariot that rises above the palace, the bodies of the two*
> *children visible next to her.*

MEDEA

> Why all the noise? Why are you hammering at the doors?
> You're a little late to be looking for your family.
> You can say what you want from where you stand,   1320

but you'll never reach us now.
This is the chariot of Helios, my grandfather,
sent to save us from our enemies.

JASON

You abomination!
Loathed by the gods,
by me, and by all mankind!
That you, a mother, could lift your sword
to your little ones and leave me childless . . .
After such sacrilege, how will you dare
to face the sun and earth?
How could I not have seen the beast inside you?
I am sane at last, but I was mad before.
Mad to bring a barbarian into Greece: 1330
toxic, black with plague, already traitor
to your father and your native land. A living curse:
but the gods have turned *your* punishment on *me*!

You killed your little brother
the day you stepped aboard the *Argo*:
you walked his blood across the decks.
That's how you began.
After marrying me, and bearing my children,
you kill them too—because of sex and the marriage bed,
out of jealousy and spite.
No Greek woman would have thought of doing such
    things;   1340
I ended up with you,

71

and what a disaster it has proved.
To take that hand in marriage,
the hand that has done all this!
To choose a lion bitch over a woman:
a thing more savage than the brutal Scylla!
But what's the use? Ten thousand curses
would not dent your metalled heart.
Go on to Hell, child-butcher, she-witch!
Leave me to mourn my wreckage.
My new-found bride.
The sons that I will never hold alive again.
All of this lost. I have lost them all.   1350

MEDEA

I could reply to each of these,
but Zeus the father knows
what services I rendered you
and how you have repaid me.
If you thought you could dishonor my bed
then enjoy the rest of your days laughing about it,
you were wrong. And so was your pretty princess.
And Creon was wrong, too, if he thought
he could just brush me away into exile.
Call me what you want—savage, lioness, witch—
I know that I have split you open,
and reached your heart with this.   1360

JASON

And split yourself: you must share some pain . . .

72

MEDEA

Your pain is a comfort to mine. You will never mock me
now.

JASON

Children, you had evil as a mother!

MEDEA

Children, your father's treachery brought this all on you.

JASON

It was not my hand that killed my sons.

MEDEA

No, it was your lust, and the insult of your new marriage.

JASON

You think it is right to murder your children over a *marriage*?

MEDEA

You think such an insult trivial, to a woman?

JASON

To a sane one, yes. But you find insults everywhere.

MEDEA

Your sons are dead. How does *that* feel?   1370

JASON

They live on as spirits, who will haunt you to Hell.

MEDEA

The heavens know who started this.

JASON

They know your evil heart.

MEDEA

Hate on! I am so sick of your pathetic voice.

JASON

And I am heartsick of yours. I would never hear it again.

MEDEA

Willingly. What are your last words to me?

JASON

Allow me my dead children—
to bury them in peace, and mourn them.

MEDEA

No. I will bury them myself.
These hands will take them to the temple of Hera Acraea
where no enemy will violate their graves.   1380
I'll found a holy festival, with sacrifices,
in expiation of these acts. And after that,
I'll go to Athens, city of Erectheus,

to live with King Aegeus, son of Pandion.
But you, as is fitting, will be shown a coward's death:
you will be killed by a piece of rotting timber,
falling from the wreck of your blessed *Argo*.
A bitter end to your bitter life with me.

JASON

Then I call on the Fury of vengeance,
and the agents of Justice, to cut you down.   1390

MEDEA

What god or higher power would listen to an oath-breaker
  and liar?

JASON

Filth! Child-murderer!

MEDEA

Go back and bury your bride.

JASON

I came here a father, and go home childless.

MEDEA

Your grief is just beginning. Wait until you're old.

JASON

Oh my children, dear sons.

MEDEA

Dear to their mother, not to you.

JASON

So dear you killed them?

MEDEA

That you might die of grief.

JASON

Let me just touch them once more:
hold them in my arms and kiss them one last time.   1400

MEDEA

You rejected them, sent them into exile,
and now you want their kisses?

JASON

One last time . . .

MEDEA

No. You waste your breath.

JASON

Zeus, do you hear? She denies me even this!
Mocked, rejected, driven away—
by a beast fouled with the blood of children.
With all my strength, Medea,
with all the life that's left to me,

I'll lament this dreadful day, and call the gods   1410
to witness that you killed my sons
and now refuse to let me touch or bury them.
Oh gods, I wish I'd never bred these boys,
or lived to see them dead—
or seen you *ever*,
and never climbed into your lethal bed.

Medea with the corpses of her children disappears from view.
Exit Jason.

CHORUS

Zeus has all things in his power,
and has the power to confound.
What mortals hope, the gods frustrate.
From our dull lives and loves they make
an unexpected passion play.
They turn the bright air black,
turn our dreams back to nightmare.
And that is what has happened here today.

GLOSSARY

AEGEUS (**eej**-yooss), king of Athens and the father of Theseus.

APHRODITE (af-ruh-**dy**-ti), daughter of Zeus, the goddess of love and beauty.

APOLLO (uh-**pol**-oh), son of Zeus and Leto, the god of prophecy, music, medicine and poetry, sometimes identified with the sun.

ARTEMIS (**art**-im-iss), daughter of Zeus and Leto, the virgin goddess of the hunt and the twin sister of Apollo.

ATHENS (**ath**-uhnz), the main settlement in Attica, in central Greece. It has been the capital of the country since 1832.

CEPHISUS (**kef**-i-suhss), a river flowing through the Athenian plain.

CLASHING ROCKS, also known as the Blue Rocks, or the Symplegades (sim-**pleg**-uh-deez), two floating cliffs that swung together and crushed any ship that attempted passage of the Bosphorus until the hero Jason managed it by trickery, allowing the *Argo* to pass safely through, after which the rocks became fixed, and Greek access to the Black Sea was opened. Pliny suggests they are the Fanari Islands.

COLCHIS (**kol**-kiss), an ancient region on the Black Sea, south of the Caucasus Mountains, ruled by Aeëtes, Medea's father. It was the site of Jason's legendary quest for the Golden Fleece. Now mostly the western part of Georgia.

CORINTH (**korr**-inth), a city of southern Greece in the northeast Peloponnese on the Gulf of Corinth. In 1858 the old city (today a town 3 km southwest of the modern city) was totally destroyed by an earthquake. The new city of Corinth was founded on the coast of the Gulf of Corinth.

CREON (**kree**-on), king of Corinth.

DELPHI (**del**-fy), an ancient town of central Greece near Mount Parnassus, and the site of a famous oracle of Apollo.

DIONYSUS (dy-uh-**ny**-suhss), son of Zeus by Semele, god of vegetation and fruitfulness, known especially as the god of wine and ecstasy.

ERECTHEUS (i-**rek**-thyooss, i-**rek**-thi-uhss), an early king of Athens.

EROS (**eer**-oss), the god of love, son of Aphrodite.

FURIES, the three terrible winged goddesses with serpentine hair: Alecto (unceasing in pursuit), Megaera (jealous) and Tisiphone (blood avenger), who pursue and punish perpetrators of unavenged crimes, hounding their victims until they die in a "furor" of madness or torment.

HARMONIA, the immortal goddess of harmony and concord.

HECATE (**hek**-uh-ti), an ancient fertility goddess who later became associated with Persephone as queen of Hades and protector of witches.

HELIOS (**hee**-li-oss), the sun god, son of Hyperion, depicted as driving his chariot across the sky from east to west daily.

HERA (**heer**-uh), the queen of the gods and the consort of Zeus, goddess of women, marriage and childbirth.

HERA ACRAEA (uh-**kray**-uh), the goddess of the hilltops; her temple is sited between Lechaeon and Pagae on the Gulf, across the water from Corinth.

HERMES (**hur**-meez), the god of commerce, invention, cunning and theft, who also served as messenger, scribe and herald for the other gods.

INO (**y**-noh), daughter of Cadmus. Driven mad by Hera, she jumped into the sea with her children.

IOLCOS (y-**ol**-kuhss), Jason's native town, near Mount Pelion in northeast Greece. Today Iolcos is a small village.

JASON (**jay**-suhn), the leader of the Argonauts. He was the son of Aeson, king of Iolcos in Thessaly. Raised by Chiron after his father's half-brother Pelias seized Iolcos, he returned as a young man and was promised his inheritance if he could bring back the Golden Fleece.

JUSTICE, goddess of Justice, usually known as Dike (**dee**-kay).

MAIA (**my**-uh), a goddess, the eldest of the Pleiades.

MEDEA (muh-**dee**-uh, mi-**dee**-uh), princess of Colchis, skilled in magic and sorcery. Hera made her fall in love with Jason and she helped him, against the will of her father, Aeëtes, to obtain the Golden Fleece.

MOUNT PELION (**pee**-li-uhn), a mountain in northeast Greece, in eastern Thessaly. According to Greek legend, it was the home of the centaurs, especially Chiron. Today, Mount Pelion is part of the prefecture of Magnesia.

ORPHEUS (**or**-fi-uhss, **or**-fyooss), a legendary Thracian poet and musician whose music had the power to move even inanimate objects and who almost succeeded in rescuing his wife Eurydice from Hades.

PANDION (**pan**-di-uhn), an early king of Athens, grandson or great-grandson of Erectheus.

PEIRENE (py-**ree**-ni, pay-**ree**-ni), a fountain or spring in Corinth. It was said to be a favored watering hole of

Pegasus, a place sacred to the Muses, and a source of inspiration to poets.

PELIAS (**pee**-li-ass), uncle of Jason, usurper of the throne of Iolcos. He was the son of Tyro and Poseidon and the twin brother of Neleus. After his birth his mother married Cretheus, king of Iolcos, and gave birth to Aeson, Jason's father. After Cretheus' death Pelias seized power, killed (or imprisoned) Aeson and exiled Neleus. Later Medea, hoping to restore Jason as rightful successor to the throne, tricked the daughters of Pelias into murdering him.

PIERIAN SPRING (py-**eer**-i-uhn), a spring in northern Thessaly, sacred to Orpheus and the Muses.

PITTHEUS (**pit**-thi-uss, **pit**-thooss), king of Troezen, a son of Pelops and father of Aethra, Theseus' mother. He was a wise man and understood the words of Aegeus' prophecy when no one else did.

SCYLLA (**sil**-uh), a six-headed female sea monster who lived in a cave opposite Charybdis and devoured sailors.

SISYPHUS (**siss**-if-uhss), a cruel king of Corinth; known for his avarice, deceit and violation of the laws of hospitality, he was condemned forever to roll a huge stone up a hill in Hades only to have it roll down again on nearing the top.

THEMIS (**them**-iss), a Titan; sometimes identified as an earth goddess, she was more commonly a goddess of law, order and justice.

TROEZEN (**tree**-zuhn), the birthplace of Theseus. A small town in the northeastern Peloponnese, near Epidaurus, southwest of Athens and a few miles south of Methana. Now known as Troizina.

ZEUS (zyooss, zooss), the principal god of the Greek pantheon, ruler of the heavens, and father of other gods and mortal heroes.

ACKNOWLEDGMENTS

This translation was made in Rönnäs, Dalarna; my thanks go to Eva Sack-Barriga.

I am grateful to Rachel Cugnoni and Rosalind Porter at Vintage, and particularly to Elizabeth Foley, who commissioned the book, and whose close reading against the Greek original was enormously helpful.

ABOUT THE AUTHOR
AND TRANSLATOR

EURIPIDES is thought to have lived between 485 and 406 BC. He is considered to be one of the three great dramatists of Ancient Greece, alongside Aeschylus and Sophocles. He is particularly admired by modern audiences and readers for his astute and balanced depiction of human behavior. *Medea* is his most famous work.

ROBIN ROBERTSON is from the northeast coast of Scotland. He has received a number of honors for his poetry, including the E. M. Forster Award from the American Academy of Arts and Letters. His third book, *Swithering,* won the 2006 Forward Prize for Best Collection. He lives and works in London.